Drip. Drop.

Will a raincoat and an umbrella keep her dry?
What will Molly do *now*?

Will Molly get wet?

She puts up an umbrella.

Molly puts on a raincoat.

Molly wants to go outside.

It is still raining.
Drip. Drop.

What will Harvey do now?

Will a tie keep him dry?

Will Harvey get wet?

Harvey puts on a tie.

What should Harvey put on?

Harvey wants to go outside.

It is still raining.
Drip. Drop.

What will Gail do now?

Will mittens keep her dry?

Will Gail get wet?

Gail puts on her mittens.

What should Gail put on?

Gail wants to go outside.

It is still raining.
Drip. Drop.

What will Cliff do now?

Will a hat keep him dry?

Will Cliff get wet?

Cliff puts on a hat.

What should Cliff put on?

Cliff wants to go outside.

It is raining.
Drip. Drop.

Library of Congress Cataloging in Publication Data

Gordon, Sharon.
    Drip drop.

    Summary: Four children try to decide what to
wear outside on a rainy day.
    [1. Rain and rainfall—Fiction.   2. Clothing
and dress—Fiction]   I. Page, Don.   II. Title.
PZ7.G65936Dr   [E]   81-5112
ISBN 0-89375-507-9 (case)   AACR2
ISBN 0-89375-508-7 (pbk.)

Drip, Drop

Written by Sharon Gordon

Illustrated by Don Page

Troll Associates

A Giant First-Start Reader

This easy reader contains only 38 different words, repeated often to help the young reader develop word recognition and interest in reading.

Basic word list for *Drip, Drop*

a	her	raincoat
an	him	raining
and	is	she
Cliff	it	should
do	keep	still
drip	mittens	tie
drop	Molly	to
dry	now	umbrella
Gail	on	up
get	outside	wants
go	put	wet
Harvey	puts	what
hat		will